Daniel Plays at School

adapted by Daphne Pendergrass
based on the screenplay "Problem Solver Daniel"
written by Becky Friedman
poses and layouts by Jason Fruchter

Ready-to-Read

Simon Spotlight
New York   London   Toronto   Sydney   New Delhi

SIMON SPOTLIGHT
An imprint of Simon & Schuster Children's Publishing Division
1230 Avenue of the Americas, New York, New York 10020
This Simon Spotlight edition July 2016
SIMON SPOTLIGHT, READY-TO-READ, and colophon are registered trademarks of Simon & Schuster, Inc.
For information about special discounts for bulk purchases, please contact Simon & Schuster Special Sales at
1-866-506-1949 or business@simonandschuster.com.
Manufactured in the United States of America 0516 LAK
2 4 6 8 10 9 7 5 3 1
ISBN 978-1-4814-6103-0 (hc)
ISBN 978-1-4814-6102-3 (pbk)
ISBN 978-1-4814-6104-7 (eBook)

"Do you want to play?" asks Miss Elaina.

"What should we do?"
We ask Teacher Harriet.

Prince Wednesday wants to play with us!